We Can Do It!

HELPING WITH DINNER

By Lois Fortuna

Gareth Stevens
PUBLISHING

Please visit our website, www.garethstevens.com. For a free color catalog of all our high-quality books, call toll free 1-800-542-2595 or fax 1-877-542-2596.

Library of Congress Cataloging-in-Publication Data

Fortuna, Lois, author.
Helping with dinner / Lois Fortuna.
pages cm. — (We can do it!)
Includes index.
ISBN 978-1-4824-3811-6 (pbk.)
ISBN 978-1-4824-3829-1 (6 pack)
ISBN 978-1-4824-3830-7 (library binding)
1. Cooking—Juvenile literature. I. Title.
TX652.5.F654 2016
641.5—dc23
2015028846

First Edition

Published in 2016 by
Gareth Stevens Publishing
111 East 14th Street, Suite 349
New York, NY 10003

Editor: Ryan Nagelhout
Designer: Laura Bowen

Photo credits: Cover, pp. 1, 5, 7, 9, 11, 13, 17, 19, 21, 23, 24 (noodles and salad) Oksana Kuzmina/Shutterstock.com; pp. 15, 24 (vegetables) Jimmy Yan/Shutterstock.com

Printed in the United States of America

CPSIA compliance information: Batch #CW16GS: For further information contact Gareth Stevens, New York, New York at 1-800-542-2595.

Contents

It's fun to help
with dinner.

My family
is making pasta.

I help stir
the noodles.

I use a spoon.
It is made of wood.

I help make a salad.

It is made of plants called vegetables.

We add a
leafy vegetable.
This is called lettuce.

My mom helps me
cut cucumbers.

We put oil on it.
This is called dressing.

Now it's time to eat!

Words to Know

lettuce

noodles

vegetables

Index